G 453580

MOIRA'S BIRTHDAY

Story by Robert Munsch
Art by Michael Martchenko

Annick Press Ltd.
Toronto, Canada M2M 1H9

© 1987 Robert Munsch (Text)
© 1987 Michael Martchenko (Art)

Seventh Printing, June 1990

All Rights Reserved

Annick Press gratefully acknowledges
the contributions of the Canada Council
and The Ontario Arts Council

Canadian Cataloguing in Publication Data

Munsch, Robert N., 1945–
  Moira's birthday

(Munsch for kids)
ISBN 0-920303-85-4 (bound) ISBN 0-920303-83-8 (pbk.)

I. Martchenko, Michael. II. Title. III. Series:
Munsch, Robert N., 1945– . Munsch for kids.

PS8576.U58M65 1987   jC813′.54   C87-094699-4
PZ7.M86Mo 1987

 Printed on acid free paper

Printed and bound in Canada by D.W. Friesen & Sons, Altona, Manitoba

To Moira Green

One day Moira went to her mother and said, "For my birthday I want to invite grade 1, grade 2, grade 3, grade 4, grade 5, grade 6, aaaaand kindergarten."
Her mother said, "Are you crazy? That's too many kids!"

So Moira went to her father and said, "For my birthday I want to invite grade 1, grade 2, grade 3, grade 4, grade 5, grade 6, aaaaand kindergarten."
Her father said, "Are you crazy? That's too many kids. For your birthday you can invite six kids, just six: 1-2-3-4-5-6; and NNNNNO kindergarten!"

So Moira went to school and invited six kids, but a friend who had not been invited came up and said, "Oh Moira, couldn't I please, PLEASE, PLEEEASE COME TO YOUR BIRTHDAY PARTY?" Moira said "Ummmmmm...O.K."

By the end of the day Moira had invited grade 1, grade 2, grade 3, grade 4, grade 5, grade 6, aaaaand kindergarten. But she didn't tell her mother and father. She was afraid they might get upset.

On the day of the party someone knocked at the door: rap, rap, rap, rap, rap, rap. Moira opened it up and saw six kids. Her father said, "That's it, six kids. Now we can start the party."

Moira said, "Well, let's wait just one minute."

So they waited one minute and something knocked on the door like this:

blam, blam, blam, blam.

The father and mother opened the door and they saw grade 1, grade 2, grade 3, grade 4, grade 5, grade 6, aaaaand kindergarten. The kids ran in right over the father and mother.

When the father and mother got up off the floor they saw: kids in the basement, kids in the living room, kids in the kitchen, kids in the bedrooms, kids in the bathroom, and kids on the ROOF!

They said, "Moira, how are we going to feed all these kids?"
Moira said, "Don't worry, I know what to do."

She went to the telephone and called a place that made pizzas.

She said, "To my house please send two hundred pizzas."

The lady at the restaurant yelled, "TWO HUNDRED PIZZAS! ARE YOU CRAZY? TWO HUNDRED PIZZAS IS TOO MANY PIZZAS."

"Well, that is what I want," said Moira.

"We'll send ten," said the lady. "Just ten, ten is all we can send right now." Then she hung up.

Then Moira called a bakery. She said, "To my house please send two hundred birthday cakes." The man at the bakery yelled, "TWO HUNDRED BIRTHDAY CAKES! ARE YOU CRAZY? THAT IS TOO MANY BIRTHDAY CAKES." "Well that is what I want," said Moira. "We'll send ten," said the man. "Just ten, ten is all we can send right now." Then he hung up.

So a great big truck came and poured just ten pizzas into Moira's front yard. Another truck came and poured just ten birthday cakes into Moira's front yard. The kids looked at that pile of stuff and they all yelled, "FOOD!"

They opened their mouths as wide as they could and ate up all the pizzas and birthday cakes in just five seconds. Then they all yelled, "MORE FOOD!"

"Uh, oh," said the mother. "We need lots more food or there's not going to be a party at all. Who can get us more food, fast?"

The two hundred kids yelled, "WE WILL!" and ran out the door.

Moira waited for one hour, two hours and three hours.

"They're not coming back," said the mother.

"They're not coming back," said the father.

"Wait and see," said Moira.

Then something knocked at the door like this:

blam, blam, blam, blam.

The mother and father opened it up and the two hundred kids ran in carrying all sorts of food.

There was fried goat, rolled oats, burnt toast and artichokes: old cheese, baked fleas, boiled bats and beans. There was egg nog, pork sog, simmered soup and hot dogs; jam jars, dinosaurs, chocolate bars and stew.

The 200 kids ate the food in just 10 minutes. When they finished eating, everyone gave Moira their present. Moira looked around and saw presents in the bedrooms, presents in the bathroom and presents on the roof.

"Oh-oh," said Moira. "The whole house is full of presents. Even I can't use that many presents."

"And who," asked the father, "is going to clean up the mess?"
"I have an idea," said Moira, and she yelled, "anybody who helps to clean up gets to take home a present."

The two hundred kids cleaned up the house in just 5 minutes. Then each kid took a present and went out the door.

"Whew," said the mother. "I'm glad that's over."
"Whew," said the father. "I'm glad that's over."
"Uh-oh," said Moira. "I think I hear a truck."

A great big dump truck came and poured one hundred and ninety pizzas into Moira's front yard. The driver said, "Here's the rest of your pizzas." Then another dump truck came and poured one hundred and ninety birthday cakes into Moira's front yard. The driver said, "Here's the rest of your birthday cakes." "How," said the father, "are we going to get rid of all this food?"

"That's easy," said Moira, "We'll just have to do it again tomorrow and have another birthday party! Let's invite grade 1, grade 2, grade 3, grade 4, grade 5, grade 6 aaaaaaand kindergarten."

The End